Ready For Reading!

SPRATTON C.E.
PRIMARY SCHOOL

LEVEL 2

Dear Parents,

Congratulations! Your child has embarked on an exciting journey – they're learning to read! As a parent, you can be there to support and cheer them along as they take their first steps.

At school, children are taught how to decode words and arrange these building blocks of language into sentences and wonderful stories.

At home, parents play a vital part in reinforcing these new-found skills. You can help your child practise their reading by providing well-written, engaging stories, which you can enjoy together.

This series offers exactly that, and more. These stories support inexperienced readers by:

- gradually introducing new vocabulary
- using repetition to consolidate learning
- gradually increasing sentence length and word count
- providing texts that boost a young reader's confidence.

As each book is completed, engaging activities encourage young readers to look back at the story, while a Picture Dictionary reinforces new vocabulary. Enjoyment is the key – and reading together can be great fun for both parent and child!

Prue Goodwin
Lecturer in Literacy and Children's Books

D0234554

How to use this series

This series has 4 levels. The facing page shows what you can expect to find in the books at each level.

As your child's confidence grows, they can progress to books from the higher levels. These will keep them engaged and encourage new reading skills.

The levels are only meant as guides; together, you and your child can pick the book that will be just right.

Here are some handy tips for helping children who are ready for reading!

 Give them choice – Letting children pick a book (from the level that's right for them) makes them feel involved.

Talk about it – Discussing the story and the pictures helps children engage with the book.

Read it again – Repetition of favourite stories reinforces learning.

Cheer them on! – Praise and encouragement builds a child's confidence and the belief in their growing ability.

LEVEL 1 For first readers

* short, straightforward sentences
* basic, fun vocabulary
* simple, easy-to-follow stories of up to 100 words
* large print and easy-to-read design

LEVEL 2 For developing readers

* longer sentences
* simple vocabulary, introducing new words
* longer stories of up to 200 words
* bold design, to capture readers' interest

LEVEL 3 For more confident readers

* longer sentences with varied structure
* wider vocabulary
* high-interest stories of up to 300 words
* smaller print for experienced readers

LEVEL 4 For able readers

* longer sentences with complex structure
* rich, exciting vocabulary
* complex stories of up to 400 words
* emphasis on text more than illustrations

Once you have read the story, you will find some amazing activities at the back of the book! There are Excellent Exercises for you to complete, plus a super Picture Dictionary.

But first it is time for the story . . .

Ready?
Steady?
Let's read!

Rory Tyger

Newton

LiTTLE TiGER

LONDON

CREAK! CREAK! CRE-E-EAK!

Newton woke up suddenly.
There was a funny noise in
his bedroom.

"Do not be scared," he told
his toys. "It was only the
wardrobe door!"

FLAP! FLAP! FLAP!

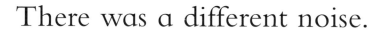

There was a different noise.

Newton got out of bed.
He tiptoed towards the sound.
"Of course!" he said . . .

"It was my curtains flapping in
the breeze!"
Newton closed the window.

SPLISH!

SPLASH!

SPLOSH!

Another noise!

He looked out.
    The noise was not
coming from outside.

And it was not
coming from
the bedroom.

"I am going to
look around,"
he told his toys.

Newton crept down
the corridor.

SPLISH!
SPLASH!
SPLOSH!

There was the noise again.

He opened the
bathroom door.

"It is the tap!" said Newton.

He turned it off
and went back to bed.

It was very quiet for a moment.
But then . . .

RUMBLE!
RUMBLE!
RUMBLE!

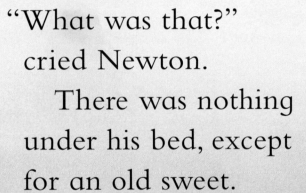

"What was that?"
cried Newton.
    There was nothing
under his bed, except
for an old sweet.

Newton listened.

RUMBLE!
RUMBLE!
RUMBLE!

Suddenly, he
knew what
was making
the noise!

He went into the kitchen and
got something to eat.

Now it was quiet because . . .

. . . the rumbling had
   been his empty tummy!

"There is always an
  explanation for everything,"
  he told his toys. "Goodnight!"

SNORE!
SNORE!
SNORE!

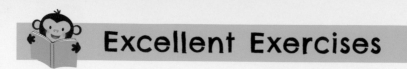

Have you read the story? Well done!
Now it is time for more fun!

Here are some questions about the story. Ask an adult to listen to your answers, and help if you get stuck.

Brave Bear

In this story, Newton gets out of bed to find out what is making funny noises. Can you think of a time when *you* were brave?

Favourite Food

Can you see what Newton has made himself to eat and drink in this picture? What is *your* favourite snack?

Top Teddy

Now describe what Newton is doing in this picture.

Night Noises

Can you remember what was making the funny noise
at the very end of the story? Do *you* know anyone who
makes that noise?

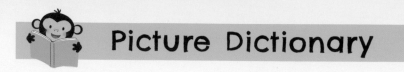

Picture Dictionary

Can you read all of these words from the story?

crept

curtains

listened

scared

sweet

toys

tummy

window

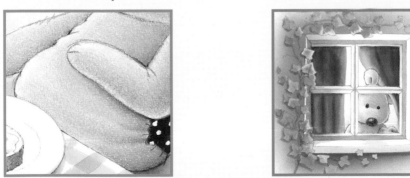

Can you think of any other words that describe these pictures – for example, what colours can you see? Why not try to spell some of these words? Ask an adult to help!

Hopping Mad!

Fred has five frogs. Finn has five frogs, too. And when ten frogs get together, it is party time! But Fred and Finn do not find the froggy madness very funny . . .

Ouch!

Hedgehog is about to go to sleep when OUCH! an apple lands on her back! Will her friends be able to help her?

Where There's a Bear, There's Trouble!

Where there's a bee there's honey. So when Bear spies a bee, he chases after it. But, where there's a bear, there's trouble. So the bee buzzes off as fast as it can . . . !

The Wish Cat

Holly wants a cute little kitten more than anything else in the world. But when she wishes on a star, she ends up with a scruffy cat instead!

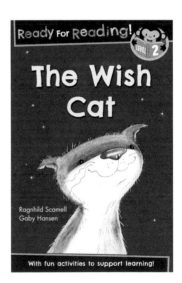

For Connie and Christien, Thomas And Dominic and Mrs Murphy — R T

LITTLE TIGER PRESS LTD,
an imprint of the Little Tiger Group
1 The Coda Centre, 189 Munster Road, London SW6 6AW
First published in Great Britain 2001
This edition published 2017
Text and illustrations copyright © Rory Tyger 2001, 2013
Artwork arranged through Advocate
All rights reserved
Printed in China
978-1-84869-736-2
LTP/1800/1856/0417
2 4 6 8 10 9 7 5 3 1

More books from Little Tiger Press!